THE JOURNEY OF MASTER CHANG

ROGER COCKREHAM

To order additional copies of this book, contact:
Xlibris
844-714-8691
www.Xlibris.com
Orders@Xlibris.com

ISBN:	Softcover	978-1-6698-3996-5
	EBook	978-1-6698-3995-8

Print information available on the last page

Rev. date: 08/16/2022

For

Liam, Christopher, and Jacob

PROLOGUE

It was a quiet time
When there was virtue.
The journey of Master Chang
Was a journey of virtue.

1

CHAPTER

Honesty & Humility

Honesty is not
Doing only the right thing;
But with great kindness.

It was a clear cool morning when Master Chang left his small home called Swinging Bridge, overlooking a small but fast moving stream beneath the towering mountains. Master Chang had lived in the little valley for most of his life, and until recently, the only way out was across the stream on an old log that would not support his great weight. But now there was a new bridge, a much larger and stronger log, provided by his friends, the Beaver family from upstream. This would make it much easier to cross the stream because Master Chang had grown much in the fifty years he had lived in the valley, and he needed the strength and width of the new log bridge to move across the stream.

You see, Master Chang was a very large Land Turtle, a painted Land Turtle, and he was very old and very wise. Over the years, many had come to see him in his clean, dry cave home in the side of the mountain above the stream. They had come seeking answers to questions about the earth, heaven, and how they should live their lives. But Master Chang was a humble Turtle, and all he did was ask questions. He did not pretend to be more than who he was. So, though he told them nothing, all went away filled with the wonder of his humility, and his wisdom.

Now, in his seventieth year, Master Chang had decided to take a long journey, back to where he was born. He thought his time had been well served, even though his advice had not always been taken. He knew that everyone thought differently, and what would be good for one would not be necessarily good for someone else. He preferred to let everyone settle their own problems. He just enjoyed helping them. His words had always been graciously received, but there were some that were very proud, and had refused to heed his advice. For Master Chang, it was not just the thought that mattered, but the action of the thought that made it complete. After all, what purpose was served if one had a good thought, given freely to someone else, only to have it thrown off, as if it were merely a leaf floating on the wind. And Master Chang had always felt that his purpose was to serve others. So now, he would leave his home, and return to where he had begun, to end his life quietly, in obscurity, his thoughts and words, what he had learned from life, dying with him.

As he crossed the bridge, Master Chang leaned heavily on his wooden staff, his flowing robes of blue and green silk barely covering the soft warm colors of his shell, which were copper and gold and green and blue. Sometimes, you could not tell if you were seeing his shell or his robes. Though he was distinctive and more colorful than most, he did not think about his appearance. It did not concern him. Master Chang had lived his life in great humility, and in moderation. He carried with him all that he owned, his staff, a small satchel of his writings, a water flask, and a small rolled up blanket for cool evenings. Wrapped inside the blanket was a small amount of food for a day or two of travel. After that, he would do as he could.

Master Chang had grown large because of his age, not his diet. He ate sparingly, but sufficiently. He had lived much longer than usual for a Painted Turtle, so that being old and a Turtle caused him to move even more slowly than usual. He was amused, as were his friends, at his slowness. But then again, this did not concern him either, because he had great patience. He was not in a hurry. Amusingly, he thought, a Turtle in a hurry was one of the great contradictions of nature. At that moment, still crossing the bridge, his constant smile grew even wider.

Maybe that was the problem, he thought. He was always happy, with a smile on his face. It could be that he wasn't taken seriously because of his smile. Could it be that the words were sufficient, but his presentation appeared foolish? That might explain why his advice was sometimes not followed. Who would take seriously someone who smiled when delivering words of wisdom? Though he did not take himself seriously, he was very serious about his life's work, and he could not help feeling, and showing, how happy he was. It was the very nature of his being.

As he was about to leave the bridge, Master Chang began to think back to when he first arrived in the little valley, so many years before. The creaking, swinging log had not swayed as much as he had thought it might, and he was not afraid of its movement. It had moved gently back and forth, and he had taken the time to watch the water move over the stones in the stream below. The constant movement of the log and the water hypnotized him, leaving him under a spell that lasted the rest of his life. The spell was a vision of the water, always in motion, never-ending, yet always changing. It flowed ever onward, despite all the obstacles in its path, over and around stones of all sizes and past the reaching branches of the trees, leaving part of itself to seep into the ground and become one with the earth, then into a quiet pool, until at the end of one's life, reached the sea and began a new one. He was in awe of its beauty, its simplicity, and its obvious symbol of life.

There were no others in the valley when he first came. But now he had friends who also lived along the steam. It was the kind of place he could call home, where he could tend his small garden, drink from the stream, and live happily. He felt fortunate that he could find his place in the world while still so young. Others of his kind traveled about, seeking fame and fortune. But Chang, (as he was known then, for he was not yet referred to as Master, a title he did not like) did not need, nor want those kinds of things. He merely desired peace, the ability to contribute to the world around him, and to have the time to think about, and try to understand, the purpose of his life. And he wanted to share those thoughts and feelings with others. It would be a simple life, but for someone with humility, like Chang, it would be a good life.

Humility is
Thinking of others before
Thinking of yourself.

2
CHAPTER
Compassion & Patience

I wonder if those
Who are hateful and greedy
Have any spirit
That could some way be changed
To be more compassionate.

Master Chang turned to follow the trail that led along the winding stream, up the valley, and into the hills beyond. The slowness of his walk allowed him the time to see the beauty of the valley. Everywhere he looked, there was the fluttering of leaves as the light morning breeze flowed with childish abandon through the trees. And above, there were large white clouds, sailing through the blue skies, as if they were great ships on a mighty sea. He also noticed his old friend, Win, a great Golden Eagle, soaring high above. He had known Win for many, many years, and although they had not spoken in a long time, they were still friends.

Win was always there, keeping watch over the world below, and Chang would always acknowledge his friendship, as he did now, by raising his staff in a salute to him.

The first day passed quietly, as he expected many of his days to pass. He had made his way almost to the home of the Beaver family when evening came. It was not late, but darkness came early in the secluded valley in the mountains. And it was just as well, because Master Chang was very tired. He realized that he would have to rest more often if he were going to be able to complete his journey. After a meal of dried apples and figs, he made his bed in a patch of ferns under a large maple tree. His friend, Win, settled onto a branch of the tree, high above, and Master Chang smiled with contentment. He slept quite soundly, and woke to the sound of Birds singing in the trees. Win had already flown.

Later in the morning, Master Chang arrived at the small wooden dam built across the stream by the Beaver family, the Lings. Father Fan and Mother My, and their three children, Flip, Flop, and Flap, shared their breakfast of small fish with Master Chang. Then the old Turtle, after thanking the Lings for the new log bridge with a bag of ripe figs, watched with tears of laughter as the children played tag in and out of the water. Their tail splashes sent showers over everyone, but there was laughter anyway. Fan and My apologized to Master Chang for their children's disrespectful behavior. But Master Chang said, "No, no, do not apologize. They are just enjoying life. You must remember, children are wonderful. They are smiles from the universe." With that, Master Chang and the Lings bowed to one another, and he turned to leave.

Master Chang gathered his belongings and began again, following along the edge of the long wide pond made by the dam, drying in the sun as he traveled. In the early afternoon, he stopped under an old willow tree to rest. The branches wavered in the light breeze, as the sun filtered through the thin long leaves, leaving streaks of light across his colorful sleek shell. He took a carrot from his roll for his lunch and then found a quiet cool place under the tree for a nap. He was sleeping quite peacefully when a young Bullfrog hopping from lily pad to lily pad suddenly awakened him. The young Frog wasn't stopping for very long whenever he did stop, which wasn't too often. Master Chang had never seen a Frog with so much energy. He was like the young Beavers, who seemed to be in constant motion.

Master Chang was lying quietly, near the edge of the pond, merely watching with interest, when the young Frog leaped in his direction. Not paying attention to where he was going, the young Frog landed on a large round stone at the edge of the water, face to face with Master Chang. The large smiling face of the Master, just a Frog whisker a way, startled him to the point of fright. He let out an "Aiiiaiiaaii" as his eyes grew large and wide. This caused Master Chang to laugh out loud, for a very long time. The young Frog, recovering his composure, asked, "What are you laughing at, old one?"

Finally, Master Chang managed to recover from his fit of laughter, and responded, "If you had seen your face just now, you would have almost died with laughter also."

“I was…just…a little…surprised, that’s all,” stuttered the young Frog. “It’s not everyday that one runs into such an old, old Turtle, with such an old, old face.”

Master Chang thought, ‘He is so young, with so much to learn about respect for his elders’. But still smiling, he asked, “What is your name, young Frog? And why have you been hopping about so much?”

“I am known as Hop Lee, and I was chasing my lunch.”

Master Chang eyed the slowly moving insect with the transparent blue wings, now moving back over the pond, and asked, “You mean that fat old Dragonfly that keeps flying around in lazy circles?

“Yes, that’s the one,” replied Hop Lee.

“But he moves so slowly. One with so much energy as you could surely catch such a fine fat Dragonfly,” said Master Chang.

Sheepishly, Hop Lee replied, “Well, every time I get close enough he suddenly goes the other way.”

Master Chang sighed deeply, and said, “Then maybe your way of hunting is not the best way. Do your instincts not tell you there is a better way?”

“I know, I know, I’m supposed to sit and wait, but that takes too long,” replied Hop Lee.

Master Chang turned his head and looked around the pond, “Look there, young friend. Behold the old gentleman standing in the rushes at the edge of the pond.” Some distance away there was a large Blue Heron, almost purple he was so dark, with a large crest of feathers extending back from the crown of his head, streaked with red and black. He was standing quite still, with his long curved neck arched forward, his slender beak pointed down at the water like an arrow.

"Yes, I see him. He's been standing there like that for hours," said Hop Lee.

"But it has not been hours, my young friend. He arrived here after I did, not too long ago. And he has been waiting patiently, for a fish to come by. Observe the patience he has learned, and the reward of what he practices from what he has learned." And as if by magic, at the end of the Master's words, the long neck of the great Blue Heron snapped down into the water. And when he pulled back his head, there was the flash of a wriggling silver Fish in his beak.

Master Chang could see the struggle against the natural instinct of patience in the young Frog's face as he watched the Heron. He asked, "Have you caught anything to eat today, with all your hopping about?"

Looking down, Hop Lee quietly replied, "No, I haven't".

"Then why don't you try a little patience, my young friend. I think it will serve you well." Laughingly, he added, "Oh, I must also tell you that hopping about so much can get you into serious trouble. The old gentleman, the Great Blue Heron, who fishes, also likes young Frogs for lunch."

With a resigned, but smiling, expression, Hop Lee looked at him somewhat respectfully. Although Master Chang expected more defiance from the young Frog, Hop Lee just nodded his head and said, "All right, I'll try. Thank you, sir." He paused for a moment, and then asked, "By the way, what is your name old one?"

"I am called Chang."

The young Frog's eyes got large again, and then he bowed, and said, "Thank you again, …Master Chang." With that, he turned and hopped away.

Master Chang watched as the young Frog moved to a large lily pad, underneath some large white lilies. He settled down and waited, and though the fat blue Dragonfly didn't venture his way, some large black Water Beetles strayed too close, not knowing the young Frog was around. And with the flick of his uncoiling tongue, lunch was served.

Master Chang, with his ever-present smile, gathered his belongings, and walked, ever so slowly along the edge of the pond, his friend Win, circling high overhead.

Toward evening, he passed the western end of the pond and made his way up the trail that led through the pass in the mountains. At dusk, he found a large outcropping of rock along the trail, and made a bed of dried leaves, just underneath the overhang. There, while Win sat majestically on a small juniper above the rocks, he thought and then he slept.

One must always wait
For that which is always good,
For patience is yours.

3

CHAPTER

Courage & Discipline

One must have courage
To face the fears of one's life
And overcome them.

Master Chang woke to the rustling of leaves in an old oak not far away. It seems that the wind had picked up during the night. It was now beginning to get light, as the morning sun was about to rise above the low hills in the East. He had not yet stirred from the confines of his shell, and he was not yet fully awake, when he suddenly became aware of the presence of someone else. He felt a sense of danger, but slowly he emerged, looking around the still dimly lit recess. He was now beginning to see that there was more to this little overhang than he had first thought. It now appeared that it continued further back into the rocky hill, forming a deep pocket. It was not too different from the small cave that he had enlarged into a warm comfortable home in Swinging Bridge. It was just that the opening was much larger than his cave in Swinging Bridge.

At first he saw nothing unusual, but suddenly there they were, two very small, but very intent, bright green eyes, deep within the shadows and leaves at the back of the cave-like structure. And they were staring directly at him. For a moment he held his breath, but he quickly overcame his initial sense of fear of the unknown, and confronted the stranger. Quietly, he said, "I am Chang of Swinging Bridge, I hope I have not disturbed you."

At first, there was no response, but then Master Chang saw the long slithering tongue issue from the mouth of a very large Serpent, coiled in the semi-darkness. And then he hissed, "I am Ben, the Boa, and you have entered my home without my permission."

"I am truly sorry that I have disturbed you. I shall leave so that you will be at peace," said Master Chang.

Suddenly, the large Snake uncoiled to almost his full length, putting his face within inches of Master Chang's nose. He said, "Not so fast, old Turtle. I may want you for my breakfast." He slowly lowered his body, which had been extended in mid-air over the length of the cave, down to the dry floor, starting with his tail, and ending just a few feet from his head. He moved his head to the side, but continued to look at Master Chang with an arrogant stare.

Master Chang could see that the Snake was enormous, and though Master Chang was more than four times the width of the Snake, he knew that Ben the Boa could easily crush him into a small enough size to be forced down his equally enormous mouth. And, he thought, 'I would probably be worth several meals, not just breakfast. But I'm not ready to be anyone's breakfast. I still have much to do.' To the Serpent, he said, "O great and learned Ben, as you can see, I am very large also, with a very thick and heavy shell. It would be with great difficulty that I could be crushed to the point where I could be easily swallowed. I am old and tough, and not easily broken. I know that you are a very intelligent being, and surely you can see the apparent disadvantages in making me your breakfast."

Ben the Boa, despite his nasty disposition, was indeed a very smart Snake. He was not nearly as old as Master Chang, but he had also gained wisdom with age. As he continued to weave his head back and forth in front of Master Chang, his tongue slithering in and out of his frowning face, he said, "I have heard of you, old one. You live down the valley, and dispense clever sayings to whoever will listen. But you take nothing for your trouble."

"I have no need to take anything from anyone," said Master Chang. "I have all that I need. I prefer to give to those who are in need. It makes me much happier."

Ben the Boa turned away and spoke out of the side of his mouth, with disgust in his hiss, "But if you don't take, as I do, you will have nothing, ….and that is not wise, old one."

"But I do have something, my learned friend. It is happiness. And it makes up for everything else one can possibly have. From your angry disposition, it appears that it is something you do not have, despite all that you say to the contrary. Happiness is for everyone, but there is only one way to have it. One must be generous and kind, full of charity. Otherwise, one cannot know happiness."

Angrily, Ben the Boa swung his head sharply about and snapped into Master Chang's face, "Happiness, sappiness. So much optimistic happiness has delivered you into my house. And now see what it has gotten you. You will now become a meal for me." He drew his head back a short distance, opened his mouth very wide, and was about to lunge at Master Chang when they both heard the rush of leaves and wind blowing madly into the shelter. Then the entrance to the cave suddenly got much darker.

Both turned to see an extraordinarily large Golden Eagle standing there. Ben shrunk back, and Master Chang smiled. Win only scratched the surface of the rock with his huge talons and glared at Ben. In a moment, Ben hissed, " It seems as though you have gained happiness for another day, old one," as he stared at the Eagle on his doorstep.

As he took his things and turned to go, Master Chang said, "And so have you, my friend. Your benevolence in allowing me to stay as your guest has greatly enriched my life, and, hopefully, it has yours."

Ben lowered himself to the floor of the cave, and with another frown, only hissed slowly.

"Farewell, my friend. I hope to meet you again someday," said Master Chang.

Ben glowered as Win turned and flew away as quickly as he had arrived as Master Chang waddled out of the cave and up the trail, to the west.

Ben recoiled into the back of the cave, and spent the rest of the day thinking about the Master's words. He was a very smart Snake, and so, after much thought, he finally decided that the old Turtle was right. Someday, maybe, he would be kind to someone, and give them the knowledge he had learned. That would make him happy. Maybe.

To do what is right
Takes thoughtful self-discipline
For you and others.

4
CHAPTER
Generosity & Responsibility

Generosity
Is completeness of giving;
Benefitting all.

Master Chang traveled many days without further incident, and he did not meet any one new, though he did encounter some whom he had met before. In the early morning of the tenth day, by a small stream in a high meadow, he ran into an old friend, Bag the Badger. Bag was on his way back to his den for a long day's sleep, so their visit was short, but not as pleasant as Master Chang had hoped. They had exchanged greetings, then Bag asked him why he was traveling so far from home. When Master Chang told Bag of his journey, Bag gave him a warning. "If you are going through the Mountain pass to the West, be careful My Friend. I have heard of a great Monster that lives there."

Master Chang said, " Yes, I have heard of this great Monster, but my journey lies that way. I will be careful, My Friend." With that, the two bowed to one another, and Master Chang continued his way westward.

Some days later, he was making his way through a large forest of bamboo, listening to the clacking, clunking sound of the bamboo trees, when he heard the rustling of leaves in a small clearing. When he got to the clearing, there, sitting quietly, and smiling at Master Chang, was a Giant Panda bear. It was Hsing Hsing, another old friend, with a small grin and a large paw of bamboo.

Master Chang was warned again by Hsing Hsing of the pass in the Western Mountains. They exchanged pleasentries, though Hsing Hsing was a lot like Master Chang. They didn't speak if it was not necessary. The days were colder due to the higher elevation, but he was still in the pine and bamboo forests that covered the slopes. Master Chang continued on.

I believe that the
Responsibility is
Mine, for all of us.

5
CHAPTER
Tolerance & Understanding

Tolerance is the
Acceptance of entities
Other than our own.

Master Chang had gotten to the Western Mountains by the evening, and he was looking for a place to spend the night, when he spotted a clearing in the mountain pass that was ideal for an encampment. Little did he know that he was to encamp in the one spot that was the lair of the "monster", a very large Dragon that had large green and almost gold scales and was at most a giant lizard. Master Chang had spread his blanket down when he felt the hot putrid breath of the Dragon on the back of his robe and shell. The Dragon asked, "What are you doing here?"

Master Chang turned and answered. "I want no trouble. I'm just passing through to the streams of the West."

The Dragon said, "Trouble? What trouble? I'm a poor lizard who has lost his way. I'm no trouble."

Master Chang noticed the insincerity in the dragon's voice, but said again, "I don't want any trouble. Is it all right that I camp here overnight? I will be gone first thing in the morning. Probably, before sunrise."

The Dragon said, "Yes."

Master Chang turned his back on the Dragon to put the finishing touches on his campsite, but he realized too late that was what the Dragon had anticipated. The Dragon pulled himself up to his full height and blew his breath across Master Chang. The Dragon's breath was very hot and it smelled of dead flesh, but it was not a flame, at least not yet. Master Chang pulled his robe across his shell, but the Dragon's breath became a flame and he blew it across the robe and shell. The robe caught fire and burned his shell, but it protected him. Master Chang was no longer a resplendent painted land turtle but just a land turtle with a burned shell.

Master Chang asked the Dragon, "Why?" but he already knew the answer. It was in the Dragon's nature to do what he did. He left the area as fast as he could, which was pretty fast for a turtle. Before Master Chang could leave, he could hear the Dragon take in a deep breath to blow out a fiery blast, to kill him. But the Dragon's breath impacted a large stone near the edge of the clearing, behind which Master Chang was hiding, and he was still smoldering. Before the Dragon could make another fiery breath, Master Chang made it out of the clearing, leaving his blanket and other camping supplies behind.

He made it out with his life, although he left everything behind. He wandered down the mountain, almost in a dream. He thought he was dreaming when he encountered a human, a man much like he had heard about. The man, at first startled by him and his great size, spoke a different language, but he thought he could understand him, at least his gestures. The man was three times his size, but he was not threatening in any way, and he gestured back where he had come from as if to tell Chang where he should go. So, Master Chang walked down the mountain. It was a circuitous route, one that required him to dodge stones and trees and their roots. But he kept up the general direction that he was told by the human. And finally, he encountered a stream that was shallow, but wide. He followed it for quite a while, until it got dark. So, he made a shelter of some old branches and logs, and he slept amongst the old branches and logs until he could not sleep any longer.

He wrapped his old cloak about him, but he couldn't shake the chill that he felt. Master Chang knew it was near the end for him. He thought he could impart some of his knowledge to those that would listen, but he knew it was not to be. He would die here, still some distance from where his destination was, but not that far. So, he walked, unsteadily, to the middle of the stream and laid down. He closed his eyes, and drifted off to sleep.

And understanding
Is the key to know yourself.
There are many keys.

Printed in the United States
by Baker & Taylor Publisher Services